Penelope Pup

AND THE PANCAKE BREAKFAST

Written by Lori-Ann Jackson

Illustrated by Lana Lee

To my lovers of pancakes, Myla and Merida, my greatest inspiration

Penelope Pup wakes up early. The rug is soft and cozy.
The sun is warm and bright. "What a good morning,"
Penelope whispers. She walks over to her food bowl.
Oh no! The bowl is empty.

No worries, Penelope thinks. I can make breakfast.

First, she makes a list of ingredients she will need. Eggs, flour, milk, butter, chocolate chips. Penelope loves chocolate chip pancakes.

"Oh! I must remember the **sprinkles!**"

Just then, her friend Ilo walks into the kitchen. "Good morning, Ilo. Would you like to help make pancakes for breakfast?"

Ilo grabs a mixing bowl and a measuring cup. "We can add blueberries and pumpkin seeds," Ilo suggests.
"Anything you like," responds Penelope.

Penelope adds the ingredients to the mixing bowl. Eggs, flour, milk, butter, chocolate chips, blueberries, pumpkin seeds.
Oh, and of course, **sprinkles.**

Penelope has an idea. "Let's call Leota. She loves pancakes."

Leota is very hungry. Her tummy is rumbling loudly. She is glad her friends called her. She wanders into the kitchen with a large mixing spoon. "Hello, Penelope. Hello, Ilo."

"May I have pickles and anchovies in my pancakes?" Leota asks.

"Anything you like," responds Penelope.

Penelope adds the ingredients to the mixing bowl. Eggs, flour, milk, butter, chocolate chips, blueberries, pumpkin seeds, pickles, anchovies. Oh, and of course, **sprinkles.**

The friends mix and mix and mix. Pancake batter goes everywhere!

Jerry is the fish friend from upstairs. He shows up with the griddle. "This will make perfect pancakes for us to enjoy!" Jerry exclaims. "I love coconut and worms in my pancakes." "Anything you like," responds Penelope.

Penelope adds the new ingredients to the mixing bowl. More mixing to do. Eggs, flour, milk, butter, chocolate chips, blueberries, pumpkin seeds, pickles, anchovies, coconut, worms. Oh, and of course, **sprinkles.**

Penelope Pup has another idea.

"Let's invite more friends for pancakes!"

More friends arrive to help make pancakes for breakfast.

Everyone has a favorite way to eat pancakes.

Some ingredients are yummy to Penelope Pup.

Some ingredients are yucky! Blah!

Penelope makes a new list of ingredients to include all her friends:

eggs

flour

milk

butter

chocolate chips

blueberries

pumpkin seeds

pickles

anchovies

coconut

worms

gumballs

honey

cottage cheese

ketchup

Oh, and of course, **sprinkles!**

All friends join in. They measure, mix, and cook the pancake batter using all the ingredients.

Jerry is an expert at flipping the pancakes.

The pancakes smell weird. Some are sticky and stretchy.

Others are squishy and squirmy. There are a lot of unusual ingredients.

Penelope Pup stacks and stacks and stacks the pancakes.

There are so many pancakes that they stack all the way to the ceiling.

Soon, the friends have a leaning tower of pancakes.

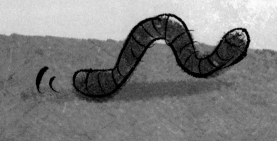

"Oh, no, look out!"
Boom!
Splat!

The pancake tower falls to the floor.

The friends feel sad. Their tummies feel empty. Penelope's tummy growls angrily but she is not angry. Instead, she smiles. " We can make new pancakes!"

Penelope makes a new list of ingredients. Eggs, flour, milk, butter.
All the friends mix, measure, and cook the pancakes on the griddle.

Penelope serves the pancakes to all her wonderful friends. She pours warm gooey syrup on top!

Fantastic friends deserve fantastic tasting pancakes. Everyone agrees.

Oh, and of course, we can't forget the **sprinkles!**

Everyone eats, and eats, and eats. Their bellies are full of fluffy pancakes, warm gooey syrup, and sprinkles!

Penelope Pup is delighted. She looks up at the clock...
It's LUNCHTIME!

Made in the USA
Las Vegas, NV
21 February 2023